D0477230

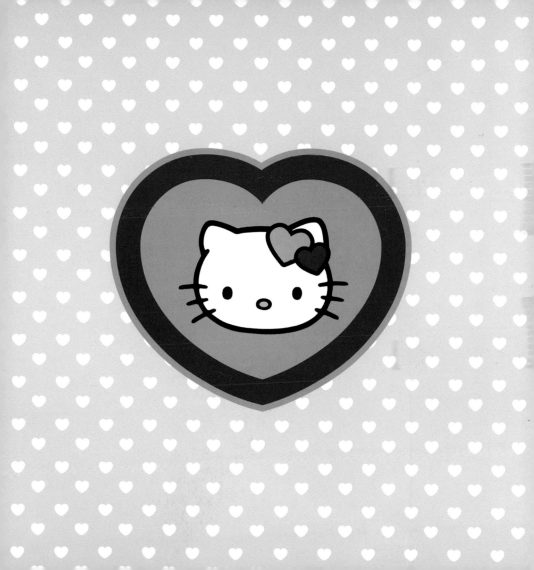

First published in the UK by HarperCollins Children's Books
in 2010
3 5 7 9 10 8 6 4 2
ISBN: 978-0-00-734490-1

A CIP catalogue record for this title is available from the
British Library. No part of this publication may be reproduced,
stored in a retrieval system or transmitted in any form or by
any means, electronic, mechanical, photocopying, recording
or otherwise, without the prior permission of HarperCollins
Publishers Ltd, 77-85 Fulham Palace Road,
Hammersmith, London, W6 8JB.
www.harpercollins.co.uk
All rights reserved

Printed and bound in China

Hello Kitty loves her boyfriend,
Dear Daniel.

Dear Daniel makes Hello Kitty
feel like dancing.

Sometimes Dear Daniel
goes far away...

...which makes Hello Kitty sad.

HELLO KITTY HELLO KITTY®

But she loves to make special cards to send to Dear Daniel...

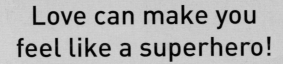

Love can make you
feel like a superhero!

Or a princess.

When you're in love, life is like
a sunny picnic in the park.

Love makes you feel like you're floating!

Even when it's raining,
it feels like summer.

When you're in love, you want to hug everyone!

Hello Kitty thinks
love is forever.